Wombat & Fox don't go looking for trouble,
but the city is a surprising place and mishaps
have a way of changing the course of their day.
These are their stories.

'This book's got everything: big waves, lots of crabs and
a sandcastle-building competition...Wombat and Fox
are my favourite holiday companions.'
Andy Griffiths

'Wombat & Fox rocks!' Andy Griffiths

A Message from Terry Denton

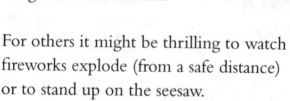

Most of us love to seek thrills.
I love hurtling down a ski run
and suddenly realising it's far
too difficult for me. I get a thrill
when I'm almost out of control
and think I'm going to fall and
break my shoulder and pop
my knees. It's scary, but it is
a good scared, mixed with
danger and excitement.

For others it might be thrilling to watch
fireworks explode (from a safe distance)
or to stand up on the seesaw.

So why am I hanging here all tied up
with rope? Well, that's another story.
Wombat and Fox can explain,
but I am not talking to either of them.

THE FIVE MONKEYS

Extremely annoying monkeys
who love annoying Fox.
Diet: Anything
anyone else is eating.
Likes: Annoying Fox.
Dislikes: Croc.

BANDICOOT

Small mouse-like marsupial
[with a built-in wallet] –
the richest fellow in town.
Diet: Oysters in gold sauce.
Likes: Making money.
Hates: Losing money.

THE HIPPO SISTERS

Twin sisters who love
any job that comes
with a uniform.
Diet: Anything, and lots of it.
Likes: Rules.
Dislikes: Rule-breakers.

Wild and Dangerous Deeds

Fox stood at the door to his apartment block.
There was a keypad where the lock used to be.
'What…?'

1

Fox looked up at Wombat's balcony.
'Help me, Wombat! I'm locked out!'
Wombat trotted downstairs to let him in.

'What happened
to the lock?'
asked Fox.
'We have a new
security system, Foxy.
We don't need a key anymore.'
'So how do we get in?'
'With a password,' said Wombat.
'Any word we like?' asked Fox.
'Any word, Foxy. We just need to pick one.'

'What about *fox*?' suggested Fox.
'Well, that could work,' said Wombat.
'We just need to press the F-O-X letters
on the keypad. Just like the numbers
and letters on your mobile phone.'
'Okay,' said Fox. 'F is number 3.
O is number 6. X is 9. So *fox* is 369.'
'If you say so,' said Wombat.
'But I think it's a bit short.'

'A bit short?'

'Yes, we need a longer pasword;
something the Five Monkeys
won't guess so easily.
'Oh,' said Fox. 'Like what?'
'966228 is a good one.'
Fox stared at his phone.

And kept staring.

And stared for
a bit longer.

'Hey!' said Fox. 'That spells *wombat*.'
'How about that!' said Wombat.
'It's a good one – easy to remember.'
'So is 369,' said Fox.
'369 is too short!'
'No, it isn't.'
'Yes, it is.'
'Isn't'
'Is.'

'Try 668 3247,' said Fox.
'What's that spell?' asked Wombat.
'*Not fair!*'

'Let's not argue, Wombat. Today is special,'
said Fox.
'You remembered?'
'Sure did! HAPPY BIRTHDAY, WOMBAT!'
'Thank you, Foxy. Is that a birthday present?'
'Well, it *is* wrapped in birthday paper, Wombat.'

Wombat ripped the paper off his present.
'A pen and a notebook!' he cried.
'Just what I wanted.'
Fox beamed.
He loved getting Wombat just what he wanted.

'How did you pay for them?'
'I saved up,' said Fox.

Actually he didn't.
Fox didn't have any money
to save. He found them both
on the newsagent's throw out pile.
The wrapping paper too.

Wombat sat at the table writing in his book.
'Are you writing about me?' asked Fox.
'No, Foxy, why would I do that?'
'No reason.'
'I am sick of boring birthdays,
 so I'm making a list of
WILD and DANGEROUS deeds
to do between now and my next birthday.'

'That's a great idea,' said Fox.
'I'm going to do that too.'
So they sat for nineteen minutes and wrote
down all the wild and dangerous deeds they
could think of.

'Finished!' said Wombat.
'Now it's time for some birthday breakfast.'

After he had his birthday porridge
and birthday cup of tea and had
taken his birthday shower and
put on his birthday suit,
Wombat was ready
to go outside.

'Now let's do all the WILD and DANGEROUS deeds on my birthday list,' he said.

'Good idea,' said Fox. 'I've got twelve wild and dangerous deeds on my list.'

'There are one hundred and one on *my* list,' said Wombat.

'Oh dear, Wombat, that's far too many for one day. Let's choose the best three.'

'Number One: Demolish an old building with explosives.'

'Wombat, no one is going to let us use explosives.'

'I guess you're right,' said Wombat.
'What about Number Two: Put my head
in a bear's jaw. That would be dangerous.'
'And just where are we going to find a bear?'
'What about Bear from across the road.'
'Possibly,' said Fox. 'But he is old and has
no teeth. That's hardly wild and dangerous.'

'Okay, Foxy, good point. We could do
Number Three: Jumping out of a plane into
the sea without a parachute.'
'Sharks, Wombat, you know I hate **SHARKS**!!'
'Okay, Foxy. What's on your list then?'

'Well,' said Fox. 'We could try getting
out of bed on the wrong side.
Who knows what could happen?'
'That's hardly wild, Foxy.'
'But it is dangerous, Wombat.'

'Forget that.
What's next on your list?'
'Number Two: Rocking back on my chair.
My mum always says it's really dangerous.'
'I'd rather jump out of an aeroplane
without a parachute, Foxy.'

'Okay, Number Three,' said Fox.
'Running with scissors.'
'Running with scissors, Foxy?'
'Really sharp scissors!'

'How about Number Four on my list?'
said Wombat. 'Riding a motorcycle
over a canyon. Now that *is* WILD
and DANGEROUS.'
'And we'll die,' said Fox. 'I don't want to die.'

Wombat checked his list.
'Number Sixty-seven?
Microwaving an egg.'
'We're out of eggs,' said Fox.
'But we've got an avocado.'
'Hardly dangerous,'
said Wombat.

'Number Seventy-eight: Scootering
down Bandicoot's Hill,' said Wombat.
'That sounds like fun.
And we might not die,' said Fox.
'We won't die, Foxy,' said Wombat.
'We might land in the duck pond though.'

'You know what water does to my fur.'
'Okay,' said Wombat. 'We scooter down
Bandicoot's Hill and stop before
the duck pond.'

'So Number Seventy-eight it is then,'
said Wombat.
'I guess so,' said Fox.
'Let's do it!' said Wombat.

Bandicoot's Hill looked
very big and very steep.

It was a quiet Sunday morning.
There were not many pedestrians.
Just the occasional duck.

Wombat looked down the hill.
'Aaahhh!' he beamed. 'The perfect
WILD and DANGEROUS birthday deed.'
'Stupid and insane!' said Fox.
'I'm not scootering down this hill.'
'But it's my birthday, Foxy. I can't do my
wild and dangerous deed on my own.'

Fox took
a deep breath,
closed his eyes,
straightened his cape
and breathed out slowly.
'I'll do it for you, Wombat,'
he said. 'But I'm not getting wet.
I don't want to ruin my new cape!'
'Okay, we'll stay out of the pond,' said Wombat.
'Now here's the deal: I steer and you brake.'
'This scooter has brakes?' said Fox. 'Hooray!'

'When I say "brake", Foxy, you brake.'
'Got it,' said Fox, who repeated it just
    to be sure. 'You say "brake", and I brake!'

'And we stop before the duck pond.'
'Of course,' said Fox. 'I DO know how
    to ride a scooter, Wombat!'

'Okay, Foxy. Ready.'
    Fox stuck up
    both thumbs.
'Set.'
    Fox nodded.
'GO!'
Wombat scootered.
'Nooo!' cried Fox
    as he jumped off.
Wombat braked.

'What happened, Foxy?'
'Sorry, Wombat! If I'm going to do this
wild and dangerous deed, I need protection.'

Fox ran home and returned completely
wrapped in pillows.

'Okay, Foxy, are you ready?'
said Wombat.
'Yep!'
'Set.'
'Set,' repeated Fox.
'GO!!'

'NNOOO!' cried Fox,
jumping off again.

'What is it this time?'
asked Wombat.
'I need my lucky troll,' said Fox.
And he ran back home to get it.

'You got your lucky charm?' asked Wombat.
Fox held up his leg.
'It's on my braking foot,' he said.
'Good idea, Foxy.'

'All set this time, Foxy?'
'Aye, aye, Captain Wombat.'

'Okay, countdown time,' said Wombat.
'Are you sure you don't just want to
step on cracks instead?' asked Fox.

'READY?'
'Ready,' said Fox.
'SET!'
'GO!'
Fox tried to jump off,
but Wombat held him
tight and they scootered
down the hill.

'YEAHHH!'
shouted Wombat.
'NOOOOO!' shouted Fox.
'Feel the wind in your fur,' said Wombat.
Fox's cape flew out behind him.
He stood up tall.
'Superfox!' he said under his breath.

Rabbit was halfway across the path,
when she heard a noise and looked up.
Wombat and Fox were hurtling towards her.

She tried to run,
but her feet
wouldn't move.

She tried to scream,
but her voice
wouldn't make
a sound.

Poor Rabbit froze
with fear.

'Watch out, Rabbit!' yelled Fox.
'BRAKE!' said Wombat.
Fox fumbled with his feet.
They wouldn't go where he wanted them to.

'BRAKE!'
cried Wombat.
Fox untangled his feet.

'BRAKE, FOXY!'

Fox pressed hard on the brake pedal.

SCREEEEEEECH!!!

They came to a stop
just in front of Rabbit.

'Rabbit! Are you okay?' asked Wombat.
'Milk! Must get milk,' said Rabbit.
She was very confused.
'We'll take you to the shop,'
said Wombat.

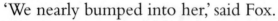

'Milk!' was all Rabbit
would say.
So they put her
on the scooter,
and continued down the hill.

'We nearly bumped into her,' said Fox.
'But we didn't,' said Wombat.
'I braked just in time, didn't I?' said Fox.
'That was teamwork, Foxy.'
'And my lucky troll, Wombat.'

As they scootered down the hill,
Rabbit woke from her trance.
She clung to Wombat's fur.
Fox felt the wind ruffle his cape.

'Eeeek!' cried Rabbit.
The Twenty Little Penguins were
crossing the road in front
of the speeding scooter.
The Twenty Penguins made
a long line; too long
a line to go around.
And too high
to go over!

**'Watch out,
Penguins!'**
yelled Fox.

'Brake!' yelled Wombat.
Fox braked as hard as he could.
No foot fumbles this time.
They screeched to a stop in front of the
Penguins, who had gathered into a huddle.

'What's up, Penguins?'
'We're in a hurry.'
'What hurry?'
'Sixteen and Seventeen need to go
to synchronised swimming classes,'
said Big Penguin.
'And they're late,' said Nine.
'Very late,' added Twelve.

'Hop aboard, Sixteen and Seventeen,
and we'll take you to the bottom
of the hill,' said Wombat.
They didn't need to be asked twice.
But Wombat asked them twice anyway.
'Come on, Penguins.'

Sixteen and Seventeen
held onto Fox,
and they all scootered
down the hill.

'We're not going to fall into that
duck pond, are we?' said Penguin Seventeen.
'Don't worry, Penguins. We're expert
stoppers, Fox and I.'
And to prove his point,
Wombat gave Fox a wink.
'Brake!' he called.
And Fox slammed
on the brakes.
The scooter came
to a quick stop.

'That's teamwork, Foxy!'
'And my lucky troll, Wombat.'

They continued down the hill.
'I love the feeling of the wind
in my fur,' said Wombat.
'I love the way my cape flaps
out behind me,' said Fox.
'I'm flying,' said Wombat.
'This is WILD and DANGEROUS!'

'Happy birthday, Wombat,' said Fox.

They flew through the roundabout,
over the kerb and onto the jetty.

Fox was ready on the brake.
'Wait for my call, Foxy,' said Wombat.
It was a short jetty.

'BRAKE!'

yelled Wombat.
Fox panicked.
His lucky troll
got stuck under
the brake pedal.

'BRAKE!'

yelled Wombat.

Fox couldn't press the brake pedal!

'BRA

KE!'

Finally Fox kicked his lucky troll
out from under the brake pedal.
He pressed hard.
The brake gripped.
The wheels screeched.
Smoke rose.

The scooter slid across
the jetty, almost to the end.
But at the very last moment,
Fox gave the brake a harder-than-hard
push and the scooter skidded to a stop.

Right at the end of the jetty.
And I mean the VERY end.
Wombat dangled over the water.
The Five Monkeys paddled
by in their blow-up raft.

'Ha! Ha! Look at the big fat fur-ball,'
  said the oldest monkey.
'Don't let go, Wombat,'
  said the second-oldest monkey.

The scooter was perfectly balanced…
Then Rabbit and the two Little Penguins
jumped off.

The scooter tipped.
'NOOO!' cried the
second-youngest monkey.
'Paddle, brothers!'

Wombat and Fox fell off the jetty and
bounced the Five Monkeys off their
raft and into the duck pond.

'Fat Wombat falling
from the sky,'
cried the youngest monkey.
'Swim for your lives,
brothers.'

Wombat and Fox floated
off across the duck pond.
'Good braking, Foxy,' said Wombat.
'Good landing, Wombat,' said Fox.
'Best birthday ever,' said Wombat.

Devil's Magic Words

Wombat and Fox stood outside
their apartment block.
'Horse,' said Wombat.
'Giraffe,' said Fox.
'Toaster.'
'Vacuum cleaner.'
'This is hopeless.'

They had forgotten the password
to their security door.
Again!

'We could wake up Moose,' said Wombat.
'Last time we did that, we got him out
of the shower,' said Fox. 'He was **not** happy.'

It was true, Wombat and Fox had locked
themselves out so many times their
neighbours were sick of letting them in.

'We could knock on Toothless Tiger's door.'
'No,' said Wombat. 'Last time he talked to us
for hours; we couldn't get away. We don't
want to go through *that* again.'

They walked around to the side of the
building. 'Our balcony's not so far up,'
said Wombat. 'We could climb.'
'You could,' said Fox. 'I'm not.'
'Come on, Foxy. We could take
it one balcony at a time. '
'Is our balcony door open?' asked Fox.
'I think so,' said Wombat. 'Give me a boost.'

Wombat climbed onto the first balcony.
He reached down and pulled Fox up.

They climbed very quietly onto the
next balcony. They didn't want to wake
Toothless Tiger.

Finally they made it to their own balcony.
The door was locked.
And so was the window.

'What about the roof?' said Wombat.
'What choice do we have?' said Fox.
Wombat boosted Fox up to the roof.

Fox reached down to Wombat.

'You are very heavy, Wombat.
What did you have for breakfast?'

'Just porridge and a banana,' said Wombat.
'And two slices of toast.
And a second helping of porridge.
And an apple. Or two. And some leftover pizza.
And two hard-boiled eggs.'

'Yes, I can tell, Wombat. You are too heavy,'
said Fox.

'Do you need a hand?'

'EEEK!' said Fox. 'Who are you?'

'Devil is the name, helping is the game,'
said the stranger.

And that is just what he did.
In the blink of an eye, he had
pulled Wombat up onto the roof.

The stranger's full name was *Tasmanian Devil*,
but that was too fancy for him.
He preferred to be called just plain Devil.

'What are you doing up here?'
'Devil has been sleeping on your roof,
 under the stars,' he said.
'How did you get in?' asked Fox.
'*We* can't even get in.'
'Devil wanders from rooftop to rooftop
 across the city. Yours was such a friendly
 rooftop, Devil decided to stay for a while.'

'Well, Devil, come downstairs and we'll make you a thank-you snack.'

Fox tried the door to the stairwell.
It was locked.

'Small matter, comrades,' said Devil.
He reached behind his ear and took
out a hairpin, which he slid into the lock.
He jiggled it about and whispered some
mysterious words.
The lock opened.

'Wow,' said Fox. 'That was like magic.'
'That's right, Fox,' he said. 'It's all in the words.'

Wombat growled. 'Huh, magic words indeed!'

Fox set out some milk and bread.
'Devil is very hungry, Fox.
Keep the bread coming,' said Devil.

Meanwhile, Wombat read
through the list he had made of
WILD and DANGEROUS deeds.

Fox sat on the balcony, sweltering in the heat.
Devil was still hungry.
So was Fox.
And Wombat too.
'Let Devil make you a treat,' said Devil.

Devil made pancakes.
He flipped them into the air and
caught them in the frying pan.

'That's clever,' said Fox.
Devil threw one right across the room.
It landed on Fox's plate.

'Let me try,' said Fox.
He flipped the pancake and it flew up in the air, but it didn't come down. It got stuck on the ceiling.

He tried again,
but the next one fell
on Wombat's head.

'You need the magic words,'
said Devil, and he whispered to Fox.

When the next pancake was ready to flip,
Fox repeated Devil's magic words.

Flipiddy diddle
Flipiddy dee
Flip this pancake
Back to me.

And, sure enough, when Fox flipped the
pancake, it did a somersault and flopped
right back into the pan.

'Did you see that, Wombat!
Devil taught me how to flip a pancake.'
'Great, Foxy,' said Wombat and returned
to his birthday list.

'There are still lots of deeds on my WILD
and DANGEROUS list,' said Wombat.
'I want to go to the swimming pool.'
'Okay,' said Fox and Devil together.
'We can try Number Eighty-eight:
The high-diving tower,' said Wombat.

'Towels.'
'Check!'

'Sunscreen.'
'Check!'

'Sunnies and hats.'
'Double check!'

'Ready!'

On the way to the pool,
Devil climbed up onto a low wall
and balanced his way along it.
Wombat was good at balancing, too.
Fox scrambled up, but fell straight off.

'Steady, comrade, try Devil's words.'
He whispered into Fox's ear.

Fox hopped up onto the wall.
Flipiddy diddle
Flipiddy dee
I'm on the wall
And the wall's under me.

Fox wobbled a few times and then
walked confidently along the wall.
'Thank you, Devil,' he said.

All three friends walked along the wall,
until Mouse scampered across their path.
She spooked Fox.
He fell off the wall.

The swimming pool was a wide, round, deep
bend in the river, with a swinging rope and
a high-diving tower.

Wombat, Fox and Devil dived into the cool water. Then they warmed up on the grass in the sun. And when they got too hot, they dived into the water again.

'It's time,' said Wombat.
'What time?' asked Fox.
'3:41,' said Wombat.
'So?'
'It's time for the high-diving tower.
Are you coming?'
'Me?' said Fox. 'Are you kidding?'
'Devil is in, Wombat.
And so is comrade Fox.'
'I am?'
'You are.'
'Oh,' said Fox.

They climbed up
the thirty-two steps
to the first level.

'This will do,' said Fox.

'No,' said Wombat. 'It has to be WILD and DANGEROUS. We have to go to the top.'

They climbed the final steps to the very top. All three crept to the edge of the tower.

'Hmmm,' said Wombat.

'Gosh,' said Devil.

'ARRRGGGHHH!!' said Fox.

'I am a wombat of WILD and DANGEROUS deeds,' said Wombat and he leapt off the tower.

SPLASH!
Devil followed close behind Wombat.

SPLASH!

They waited, but there was no third splash.

The Five Monkeys climbed the tower.
'Hurry up, Fox,' said the oldest monkey.
'You're holding up everyone else.'

'Just jump, scaredy-cat!'
 said the middle monkey.

'I don't think I want to jump either,'
 said the youngest monkey.

Wombat and Devil climbed back to
the top of the tower. Wombat growled
at the Five Monkeys.

'Jump!' said Devil.

And he bared his teeth.
He had a very impressive set of sharp fangs.
The monkeys didn't stay around
to find out *how* sharp.
All together they jumped.

Even the youngest monkey.

SPLASH!
SPLASH!
SPLASH!
SPLASH!
SPLASH!

'Now, Foxy,' said Wombat. 'Let's try again.'
Fox said nothing.

Wombat took a close look at his friend.
Fox was frozen with fear.
Not *cold* frozen.
Not just *couldn't-move* frozen.
But *frozen-to-the-spot* frozen.

Wombat shook Fox gently.

He tapped him on the cheek.
Fox didn't flinch.

Devil blew in Fox's ear.
He didn't even blink.

'Comrade Fox. I know
you can hear Devil.
He's going to give
you a little song
to break you out of this spell.'
Devil whispered into Fox's ear:
Flipiddy diddle
Flipiddy dee
Forget your fear
And look at me.

But Fox stayed frozen.

Wombat and Devil stayed with Fox
at the top of the high-diving tower.
Every now and then they tried something new.
A pinch.
A tweak of the nose.
A tickle.
A poke.
But nothing worked.

Fox was stuck on top of the high-diving tower
frozen with fear all through the afternoon.

Elephant suggested they splash water
on Fox. She let him have a whole trunk full,
but it had no effect.

Croc suggested they stand
Fox in a bucket of water.
That did no good either.

The Twenty Little Penguins suggested
they all peck him.
'That will surely wake him,'
said Big Penguin.
But it didn't.

When the sun
was setting the
Hippo Sisters
insisted Wombat
and Devil carry
Fox down to
the ground.

But getting Fox down the
very steep steps was too difficult.

'Devil has an idea,' said Devil.
'Move Comrade Fox to the edge
and everybody stand back.'

Devil stood just behind Fox and
whispered another song into his ear.

Then with a great big shove,
Devil pushed Fox off the tower.

'AARRGGGHHHH!!!'

SPLASH!

'Help, Wombat!'
cried Fox.
'Swim!' shouted Devil.
'I can't believe you pushed
him off!' said Wombat.

They hurried down the tower
and pulled Fox out of the water.
'Are you crazy!' said Fox.

'When nothing else will
work, sometimes we just
need a good push.'
'I could have died!'
'Well, you didn't. Devil knows best.'

'I'm not so sure about that,' said Wombat.

Fox was too exhausted to walk home, so
Wombat and Devil took turns carrying him.

Only they couldn't get past the security door.
'We forgot to change the password,'
said Wombat.

'Allow me,' said Devil.
He placed his head
next to the keypad.

He closed his
eyes and pressed
a few buttons.

He sang one of his
little songs and the
door swung open.

'Truly magical, Devil,' said Fox.
Even Wombat was impressed.

The next morning, when Fox ran
up to the rooftop to offer him breakfast,
Devil was gone.

'His kind are always on the move,'
said Wombat.
'But I thought he was my friend.'
'He is, Foxy. He's your
always-on-the-move friend.'

'Now sit down and have a pancake.
It's a Wombat-special.'

Superfox Saves the Day

'Look!' said Wombat.

'There's our apartment.'

'I can't see it,' said Fox.

'That's because you have your eyes closed, Foxy.'

'That's because we are very high, Wombat.'

'You're not kidding,' said Croc.
'The Five Monkeys look like ants.'
'I wish they were ants,' said Fox.
'If you think this Ferris wheel is high, wait till
you ride the Roller-coaster, Foxy.'

'I'm not ready for the Roller-coaster,'
said Fox. 'Let's try the Teacups first.'

The teacup rose gently and the whole
ride turned slowly.
'See, Wombat, this is my kind of ride.'
Fox sat back with his arms resting
on the lip of the cup.
'I can even keep my eyes open!'

The ride began to turn faster.
Fox shut his eyes.

Then the inside of their
teacup started spinning.
Fox turned white.
'Wombat!' cried Fox. 'I think
my head is about to come off.'
'Just hang on to it, Foxy,' said Wombat.

Fox held on to his head very tightly.
It didn't come off.
But his eyes nearly popped
out of their sockets.
When the ride stopped,
Fox was very giddy.
'I feel sick,' he said.

'Let's try the merry-go-round, Foxy,' said
Wombat. 'I think it will be more your speed.'
Fox stared at the horses.
Most had wild eyes
and crazy
mouths.

Finally he found one with sleepy eyes
and a smiley mouth.
The merry-go-round moved
very slowly indeed.
'This is perfect,' said Fox.
'Boring,' said Croc.
'I agree,' said Wombat.
'Let's try the Roller-
coaster next.'

They lined up at the Roller-coaster.
'It's so high I can't even see the top,' said Croc.
'No way,' said Fox. 'I'm not riding
the Roller-coaster.'
'But, Foxy!' said Wombat.
'I don't want to die,' said Fox.

'Ha! Ha! Fox is too scared to ride the Roller-
coaster,' said the oldest of the Five Monkeys.
'We heard you won free tickets,'
said the second-oldest monkey.
'Yes,' said Croc. 'I did win tickets.'
'If Fox is too scared to use them, you
should give us some of your tickets,'
said the middle monkey.
'No way!' said Croc.

'But sharing is caring,'
said the second-youngest monkey.
'When have you ever shared anything
with us?' asked Wombat.
'I gave you a cold once,'
said the youngest monkey.

Wombat, Fox and Croc ducked in to the
Tunnel of Love and climbed into a boat.

The Five Monkeys snuck in and piled into
the next boat. They are very good sneakers.

They splashed Wombat, Fox and Croc,
and threw chewed chewing gum at them.
They tried to spook them with ghost noises.
Fox knelt at the very back of their boat,
leaned out over the edge and tried
to splash them back.

Croc held tight to his cape so he didn't fall.
'Good splashing, Foxy,' said Wombat.

When the ride was finished, Wombat, Fox and Croc leaped out of the boat and ran as far away from the Five Monkeys as possible.

'Let's go on the Roller-coaster now,' said Wombat. 'Quick, while *you-know-who* aren't around.

'No,' said Fox. 'I told you, I am NOT ready for the Roller-coaster.'

So they rode the Dodgem Cars.

It didn't take long for the Five Monkeys to catch up with them. They snuck onto the ride and all squeezed into one of the empty cars.

They zoomed up behind Fox.

He turned right.
They turned right.

He turned left.
They turned left.

Then they crashed into him

THUMP!

'OWWCCHH!!' cried Fox.
'MY neck!! I think I have whiplash!'

'LEAVE MY FRIEND ALONE!'

cried Croc, and she drove her car straight
at the Five Monkeys.

BUMP!

With one mighty bump she pushed the
Five Monkeys right off the ride.

'No bumping!'

yelled the two Hippo Sisters.
They were the ride attendants and
they had very sparkly red uniforms.

'Leave the ride immediately!'

The Five Monkeys' car rolled down the hill
towards the House of Horrors.

The Hippo Sisters chased Wombat, Fox and Croc, but our friends hid behind the hot food stands.

'Your stomach is rumbling, Wombat,'
said Fox. 'The Hippo Sisters will hear it.'
'I can't help it,' said Wombat.
'I smell doughnuts.'

'Attention. Thrillseekers Park
is closing in ten minutes.'
'What!' said Fox. 'That's
not fair! We only just
got here.'

'Riding the Roller-coaster is on my birthday
list of WILD and DANGEROUS deeds,'
said Wombat.
'But the park is closing,' said Fox.
'We have to go home.'

'*WE* are not going anywhere,' said the oldest
monkey. 'We're hiding until everyone leaves.'
'Then we will have the park all to ourselves,'
said the second-oldest monkey.

'I am staying too, Foxy,' said Wombat.
'I REALLY want to ride that Roller-coaster.
It's Number Eighty-eight on my list.'

'Come on, Foxy,' said Wombat. 'It'll be fun.'

Fox took a deep breath.
He tightened his mask and shook out his cape.
'I am Superfox,' he said. 'I will stay.'

Wombat, Fox, Croc and the Five Monkeys
hid in the House of Horrors.

They waited.

And waited.

The park staff turned off the power, rolled
down the big shutters and left for the night.

'HOORAY! We have the place to ourselves,' said the Five Monkeys.

Wombat, Fox and Croc played on the rolling barrels. They laughed at each other's reflections in the trick mirrors.

When the Five Monkeys were sure the staff had gone far, far away, they opened the power box and switched on all the rides.

'I have a bad feeling about this, Wombat.'
'Relax, Foxy. It's time for WILD and DANGEROUS deeds.'
'Remember, you are Superfox,' said Croc.

All three crowded into
one of the Roller-coaster cars.

It started slowly then climbed a steep slope.
Fox gripped hard on the safety bar.

As they rolled to the top,
he closed his eyes.
They flew down the slope.
Fox screamed.

Wombat and Croc threw their arms in the air.
They stuck out their tongues.
Croc's long tongue flapped in the breeze.

They reached the bottom
and flew up the next slope,
to the very top.

'Look, Foxy,' said Wombat. 'I can see the beach.'
Fox's eyes were shut tighter than ever.

When Wombat, Fox and Croc were at the
very highest point of the Roller-coaster,
the car suddenly jerked to a stop.

'What happened?' asked Fox.

'Ha! Ha! Ha!' said the Five Monkeys from
below. 'We turned the power off.'
'Guess where you are spending the night,'
yelled the second-oldest monkey.
'Let us down,' yelled Fox.
'Sleep well,' yelled all Five Monkeys as they
clambered over the fence and ran home.

Wombat and Croc gazed out
across the lights of the city as night fell.
Fox's eyes were still closed.

'Wombat, call for help,' said Fox.
'Good idea, Foxy.'
Wombat fiddled with his phone,
then put it away.
'Well?' said Fox.
'Battery's flat!'
'This is a disaster!'
said Fox.

'We can't spend the night up here,' said Fox.
'Why not?' said Wombat. 'It's a very WILD
and DANGEROUS deed. If I'd thought of it,
I would have put it on my list.'

'Croc?' said Fox.
'Could you climb down
and get help?'

'And food,' said Wombat.
'No problem for Croc,' she said.
'I can slide down the rails.'
'You'll get splinters,' said Wombat.

Croc climbed out of the
car and onto the frame
of the Roller-coaster.

'Uh-oh,' said Croc.
'I think I'm stuck.'

'Are you all right, Croc?' called Fox.
There was no answer.

Wombat leaned over the edge of the car and
looked down. 'I think she's fallen asleep, Foxy.'

'This is a disaster,' said Fox.

'It's not a disaster, Foxy,' said Wombat. 'This is
the best WILD and DANGEROUS deed ever.'

'I'm still not opening my eyes.'
'Go on, Foxy. The view is brilliant.'
'Not listening.'
'Full moon reflecting on the water.'
'Still not listening.'
'Fireworks over the city.'
'Laa dee daaa! Laa laa!'

There was a long silence.

'We could write a note and make it into
a paper plane and throw it.'

'We have no paper,'
said Wombat.

'We could jump up and
down and yell for help.
Someone would see us.'

'There is no one about.'

'We could make my cape into a parachute.
That's it! Wombat, what do you think of that
for an idea?'

'Wombat?'

'Wombat?'

'Wombat?'

Fox sighed.
Wombat had fallen
into a deep sleep.
Such a deep snoring sleep
that nothing would wake him.

So poor Fox spent a sleepless night on the
highest point of the Roller-coaster, and he
never opened his eyes. Not even a tiny peek.
Not once.

In the early hours of the morning,
a voice called to him.
'Hello, comrade.'
'Devil, is that you?'
said Fox.

'It is the Devil indeed, the Devil you know,'
said Devil. 'What are you doing up there,
comrade Fox?'
'It's a long story,' said Fox. 'Do you have a song
to help me get down?'
'Well, it just happens that Devil does have
a song for comrade Fox.'

'*Flipiddy dee,*
Flipiddy ache,
The way to get down,
Is to take off the brake.'

'The brake!'
said Fox.
'What brake?'
He felt around his seat.
Sure enough,
he found a lever.

'Thank you, Devil!' he called,
but Devil had disappeared.

Fox opened his eyes. He blinked.
He looked down the Roller-coaster track.
'Very steep,' he whispered.

'I am Superfox,'
he said quietly.

One more look
down the track.
It was still steep.

Fox took a big breath and released the brake.
The Roller-coaster car rolled slowly at first,
but soon it was hurtling down the track.
The wind blew through Fox's fur.
His cape fluttered behind him.
Fox stood.
He stretched out his arms.
'I am king of the world!'

The Roller-coaster flew down, then up to
the top of the next peak. It rattled on, up and
down and up and down all the way to the
station, where it rolled to a gentle stop.

Fox shook Wombat.
'Wake up, sleepy head,' he said.
'Superfox has saved the day!'

And so he had.